Who Lives in the Woods?

BELL BOOKS

Who

Text copyright © 1991 by Pat Upton.
Illustrations copyright © 1991 by Karen Lee Schmidt. All rights reserved.
Published by Bell Books, Boyds Mills Press, Inc.,
A Highlights Company, 910 Church Street,
Honesdale, Pennsylvania 18431

Publisher Cataloging-in-Publication Data
   Who lives in the woods?; illustrated by Karen Lee Schmidt; by Pat Upton.
   32p.:col. ill.; cm.
Summary: Text and illustrations introduce the characteristics of animals commonly
found in the woods, including a final page of youngsters camping.
A Visual Education Book
ISBN 1-878093-19-3
1. Animals—Juvenile Literature. 2. Picture-books—Juvenile Literature. [1. Animals. 2. Picture-books.]
I. Schmidt, Karen Lee, ill. II. Upton, Pat. III. Title.
590-dc20   [E]   1991
LC Card Number 90-85721

Printed in Hong Kong

Distributed by St. Martin's Press

Lives in the Woods?

By Pat Upton

Illustrated by Karen Lee Schmidt

Who lives in the pond?

"We do," say the frogs.

Who lives in the hollow tree?

"We do," say the owls.

Who lives in the lodge?

"We do," say the beavers.

Who lives in the shells?

"We do," say the snails.

Who lives in the rocky den?

"We do," say the foxes.

Who lives in the stream?

"We do," say the jumping fish.

Who lives in the bushes?

"We do," say the deer.

Who lives in the nest?

"We do," say the birds.

Who lives in the warren?

"We do," say the rabbits.

Who lives in the web?

"We do," say the spiders.

Who lives underground?

"We do," say the moles.

Who lives in the tent?

"We do! We do!" say the campers.

"We all live in the woods."